Dear Parent:
Your child's love of reading starts here!

Every child learns to read in a different way and at his or her own speed. Some go back and forth between reading levels and read favorite books again and again. Others read through each level in order. You can help your young reader improve and become more confident by encouraging his or her own interests and abilities. From books your child reads with you to the first books he or she reads alone, there are I Can Read Books for every stage of reading:

SHARED READING
Basic language, word repetition, and whimsical illustrations, ideal for sharing with your emergent reader

BEGINNING READING
Short sentences, familiar words, and simple concepts for children eager to read on their own

READING WITH HELP
Engaging stories, longer sentences, and language play for developing readers

READING ALONE
Complex plots, challenging vocabulary, and high-interest topics for the independent reader

ADVANCED READING
Short paragraphs, chapters, and exciting themes for the perfect bridge to chapter books

I Can Read Books have introduced children to the joy of reading since 1957. Featuring award-winning authors and illustrators and a fabulous cast of beloved characters, I Can Read Books set the standard for beginning readers.

A lifetime of discovery begins with the magical words **"I Can Read!"**

Visit www.icanread.com for information
on enriching your child's reading experience.

I Can Read Book® is a trademark of HarperCollins Publishers.

The Berenstain Bears Around the World Copyright © 2016 by Berenstain Publishing, Inc. All rights reserved. Manufactured in U.S.A. No part of this book may be used or reproduced in any manner whatsoever without written permission except in the case of brief quotations embodied in critical articles and reviews. For information address HarperCollins Children's Books, a division of HarperCollins Publishers, 195 Broadway, New York, NY 10007.
www.icanread.com

Library of Congress Control Number: 2015946548
ISBN 978-0-06-235024-4 (trade bdg.) — ISBN 978-0-06-235023-7 (pbk.)

16 17 18 19 20   LSCC   10 9 8 7 6 5 4
❖
First Edition

I Can Read!

BEGINNING
1
READING

The Berenstain Bears®

AROUND the WORLD

Mike Berenstain

Based on the characters created by
Stan and Jan Berenstain

HARPER
An Imprint of HarperCollins Publishers

The Bear family is visiting

the Great Bear Museum.

Doctor Bear shows them a globe

of the Earth.

"We live right here," he says.

ATLANTIC
OCEAN

PACIFIC
OCEAN

Our
World

"It would be fun to travel

all around the world," says Sister.

"I agree," says Doctor Bear.

"Just follow me."

"Step inside my Anywhere-Anyplace

Machine," says Doctor Bear.

He pushes a button.

Everything starts to spin!

When things stop spinning . . .

they are in another country!

"Welcome to London, England,"

says Doctor Bear.

"The tower bell is called Big Ben."

"It makes a lot of noise!" says

Brother.

"Bing, bong! Bing, bong!" says

Honey.

Again Doctor Bear

pushes a button.

"Welcome to Paris, France,"

he says.

"This is the Eiffel Tower.

It is one thousand feet tall.

You can climb to the very top."

"No thanks!" says Brother.

"Switzerland is known for its clocks," says Doctor Bear, moving on. "And its mountains," says Mama.

"And cheese with holes in it,"
says Papa.

"And chocolate," say Brother
and Sister.

"Yum!" says Honey.

"In Venice, Italy, everyone travels by water," says Doctor Bear. "You need a boat to cross the street," adds Papa.

"Russia is in the far, cold north,"

says Doctor Bear.

"Its church domes are shaped

like onions."

"I don't care for onions," says Sister.

"Egypt is part of Africa,"

says Doctor Bear.

"It is the oldest country on Earth.

It is mostly desert.

But the Nile River gives it water.

Great buildings and statues of

long ago stand here still."

"Much of Africa is covered
by forest and plains,"
says Doctor Bear.

Elephant

Giraffe

Zebra

Rhino

"Look lions!" says Brother.

"Roar! Roar!" says Honey.

"Hush, Honey!" say Mama and Papa.

Cheetah

Antelope

Lion

AFRICA

"In India, we can see the sights
from the back of an elephant,"
says Doctor Bear.

"But watch out for tigers."

"Growl! Growl!" says Honey.

"Shhh!" say Brother and Sister.

"China has a long history," says
Doctor Bear.

"And a long wall!" says Brother.

"The Great Wall of China was built
to keep enemies out," says Doctor Bear.

"It's wearing me out!" says Sister.

"Australia has kangaroos,"

says Doctor Bear.

"They carry their babies in a pouch.

So does the koala.

But it looks like a teddy bear."

22

"We are near the South Pole,"
says Doctor Bear.
"Scientists and penguins live here.
But little else. It is the coldest
place on Earth."
"Brrr!" says Brother. "I'll say!"

ANTARCTICA

Anaconda

"South America is much warmer," says Doctor Bear.

"Here great rain forests are home to many animals."

Jaguar

"What animal is that?" asks Brother.

"It looks like a big beaver."

"It *is* like a big beaver.

It's a capybara," says Doctor Bear.

Tapir

Capybara

Caiman

SOUTH
AMERICA

"Now we'll visit Mexico,"
says Doctor Bear.
"Great cities were built
here long ago."

"Canada is north of Bear Country,"

says Doctor Bear.

"It's a land of great natural beauty.

Over half the lakes on Earth are here."

"Our own country is the USA,"

says Doctor Bear.

"The United States of America.

Alaska is way up north.

Here we can join a dogsled race."

"Woof! Woof!"

says Honey.

"Hawaii is an island state,"

says Doctor Bear.

"Surfers ride huge waves along

its shores."

HAWAII
USA

"A river dug out the Grand Canyon over millions of years," says Doctor Bear.

UNITED STATES OF AMERICA

George
Washington

Thomas
Jefferson

Teddy
Roosevelt

Abraham Lincoln

"The faces of presidents are
carved on Mount Rushmore.
Can you name them?"

"The Statue of Liberty
is in New York Harbor.
She stands for freedom."

"And now . . . ," says Doctor Bear,

"we are right back where we started."

The Bear family waves good-bye.

"Come back soon," says Doctor Bear.

"There are many more places to visit . . .

all around the world!"